Curious George®

The Dog Show

Adaptation by Monica Perez
Based on the TV series teleplay written by Joe Fallon

Houghton Mifflin Company
Boston 2006

For information about permission to reproduce selections from this book, write to Permissions, Houghton Mifflin Company, 215 Park Avenue South, New York, New York 10003.

Library of Congress Cataloging-in-Publication Data

Perez, Monica.
Curious George: The dog show / adaptation by Monica Perez ;
based on the TV series teleplay written by Joe Fallon.
    p. cm.
    ISBN-13: 978-0-618-72397-3 (pbk. : alk. paper)
    ISBN-10: 0-618-72397-8 (pbk. : alk. paper)
    I. Fallon, Joe. II. Title.
    PZ7.P42583Cur 2006
    2005038073

Design by Joyce White

www.houghtonmifflinbooks.com

Manufactured in China
WKT 10 9 8 7 6 5 4

George was going to a dog show.

He had not been to a dog show before.

He was very curious.

The dog show was a surprise.
The dogs were not doing tricks.
They stood.

They walked.
They ran a little.
That was all.

George visited the dogs after the show.
It was much more fun.

George loved them so much that he
wanted to take them home.

So he did.
The dog owners were busy
getting ribbons.

They did not see George leave with
their dogs.

At home George wanted to count
how many new friends he had.
It was hard work!
The dogs did not stay in one place.
George had an idea.

He put the big dogs in one room.
He put the small dogs in another room.

He put the hairy dogs in the bathroom.

Then he counted.

One . . . two . . . three hairy dogs.

One . . . two . . . three small dogs.

One . . . two . . . three big dogs.

The front door opened.

It was George's best friend.

The man was surprised to see dogs behind
every door.
"There must be twenty of them!" he said.

But George knew better.
There were three plus three
plus three dogs.
There were nine dogs in all.

The doorbell rang.
Nine dog owners had
come to get their dogs.

George waved goodbye
nine times.
What a great dog show it had been . . .
right in his own home.

rouping numbers is an important math skill. Practice looking at everyday objects with your child and then counting them in different ways. For example, you can group rocks by size or color. Some ideas for counting and grouping: the trees on the playground, the clouds, cars, pens and pencils, pots and pans, and books.

MATCH AND COUNT!

Counting by twos is often faster than counting each item if you have a lot of things to count. Match the socks below, circle each pair, and then count the pairs.

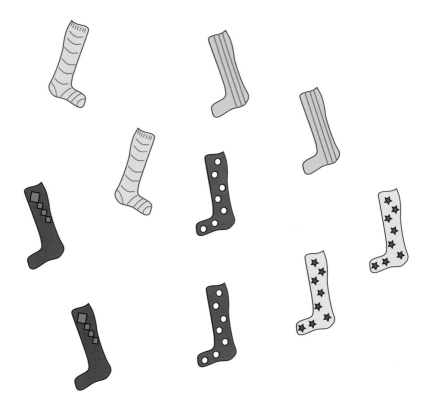